Dear Parent:
Your child's love of reading starts here!

I Can Read Books have introduced children to the joy of reading since 1957. Featuring award-winning authors and illustrators and a fabulous cast of beloved characters, I Can Read Books set the standard for beginning readers. From books your child reads with you to the first books they read alone, there are I Can Read Books for every stage of reading:

SHARED READING
Basic language, word repetition, and whimsical illustrations, ideal for sharing with your emergent reader

BEGINNING READING
Short sentences, familiar words, and simple concepts for children eager to read on their own

READING WITH HELP
Engaging stories, longer sentences, and language play for developing readers

READING ALONE
Complex plots, challenging vocabulary, and high-interest topics for the independent reader

ADVANCED READING
Short paragraphs, chapters, and exciting themes for the perfect bridge to chapter books

Every child learns in a different way and at their own speed. Some read through each level in order. Others go back and forth between levels and read favorite books again and again. You can help your young reader improve and become more confident by encouraging their own interests and abilities.

A lifetime of discovery begins with the magical words, **"I Can Read!"**

*To JoLyn Taylor-Brown
and Kent L. Brown*

HarperCollins®, 🐻®, and I Can Read Book® are trademarks of HarperCollins Publishers Inc.

Library of Congress Cataloging-in-Publication Data
Gorbachev, Valeri.
Whose hat is it? / by Valeri Gorbachev.—1st ed.
    p.   cm.—(My first I can read book)
Summary: When someone's hat blows off in the wind, Turtle asks various animals if it belongs to one of them.
ISBN 0-06-053434-6 — ISBN 0-06-053435-4 (lib. bdg.) — ISBN 0-06-053436-2 (pbk.)
[1. Hats—Fiction. 2. Turtles—Fiction. 3. Animals—Fiction.]
I. Title. II. Series.
PZ7.G6475Wk 2004
[E]—dc21
                                                                                    2003000505

❖
09 10 11 12 13 SCP 10 9 8 7 6 5

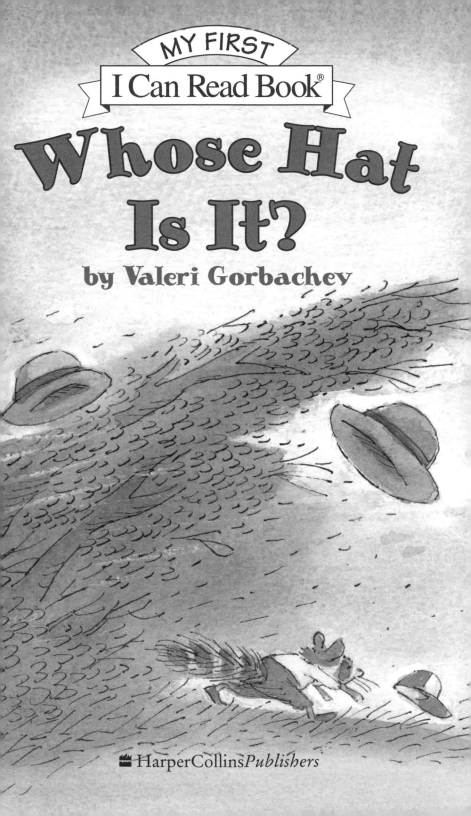

"Wow! Someone's hat
was blown off by the wind
Turtle said.

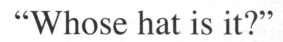

"Whose hat is it?"

"Is it your hat, Mouse?"

"It is not mine," Mouse said.

"Is it your hat, Rabbit?"

"It is not mine," Rabbit said.

"Is it your hat, Beaver?"

"It is not mine," Beaver said.

"Is it your hat, Crocodile?"

"It is not mine,"
Crocodile said.

"Whose hat is it?"

"It is mine," Elephant said.

"My hat was blown off
by the wind!"

"Thank you for finding it, Turtle!"

"You are welcome!"